Puss in Boots

| Cover illustrated by
Deborah Colvin Borgo | Adapted by
Sarah Toast | Illustrated by
Susan Spellman |

Louis Weber, C.E.O.
Publications International, Ltd.
7373 North Cicero Avenue
Lincolnwood, Illinois 60646

Manufactured in U.S.A.

8 7 6 5 4 3 2 1

ISBN: 0-7853-1856-9

Publications International, Ltd.
Story Garden is a trademark of Publications International, Ltd.

Once there was a poor miller who had three sons and very little else. When the old miller died, he left his mill to the eldest son. He left his trustworthy donkey to the middle son. The youngest son got the cat.

The youngest son was upset over his poor share. "My older brothers can work together to earn a living," he said, "but Puss and I will surely die of hunger."

The cat overheard the boy. "Don't worry," said Puss. "Just give me a sack and a good pair of boots so I can walk through the mud and brush, and you'll see that I can be a great help to you."

The boy did what the cat asked. When Puss got his boots, he pulled them on and strutted around. Then Puss put his new sack over his shoulder and walked to the edge of the woods, where many rabbits lived.

Puss picked some tender grass and thistles and put them in the sack. Then he lay down as if he were dead and waited.

A plump, young rabbit soon hopped along and smelled the fresh thistles. The rabbit knew nothing about trappers. He crawled into the bag to eat the grass and thistles.

Up jumped Puss. He grabbed the bag and went straight to the palace, where he asked to see the king.

Puss was led into the king's throne room. He made a low bow and said, "Sire, I bring you this gift from my kind master, the duke of Carabas." The king didn't know that Puss had just made up this name for the boy.

"Tell your master," said the king, "that I thank him and accept his gift with pleasure."

The next day Puss caught two partridges to present to the king. The king was pleased and said, "Thank your generous master, the duke of Carabas. He is most kind."

Every day for many weeks, Puss brought a different gift to the king. The curious king began to wonder about this mysterious duke of Carabas.

One day Puss found out that the king was taking his beautiful daughter for a drive along the river. Puss said to his master, "Go down to the river, take off your shirt and trousers, and jump in. Leave the rest to me."

The boy did as he was told. Then Puss hid the clothes under a big stone. When the king's coach came along, Puss ran into the road and cried out, "Help! Help! My master, the duke of Carabas, is drowning."

The king stopped the coach when he saw Puss. He ordered that his guards rescue the duke. The princess watched the guards pull the boy out of the river.

Puss went up to the coach. He told the king that robbers had stolen all his master's clothes and had thrown him in the river to drown.

The king wanted to help. He ordered one of his guards to quickly ride back to the palace and bring the unfortunate duke a dry, warm set of clothes.

Dressed in a fine suit of clothes, the boy did indeed look like a duke. The king's daughter certainly thought he looked handsome. When the duke of Carabas glanced at her shyly, the princess smiled back sweetly. The king saw the attraction between the two young people and asked the duke to ride with them.

Puss, meanwhile, went ahead of the royal carriage to carry out his plan. He spoke to the farmhands cutting hay in a field. "When the king comes along, you must tell him that this field belongs to the duke of Carabas. If you don't, the ogre who lives in the castle on the hill will chop you into tiny pieces!"

Sure enough, when the king drove up, he asked the farmhands who owned the land they were working. They answered, "The duke of Carabas!"

A little farther down the road, when the king asked another group of farmhands who owned the land they were working, they also said, "The duke of Carabas!" And so it went.

Everywhere the king asked, he was told that the land belonged to the duke of Carabas. The king was amazed at how much land the duke owned and how wealthy he was.

By now the princess felt she loved the duke. He, in turn, thought the princess was truly the most beautiful girl he had ever seen.

While the princess and the duke talked and got to know one another, Puss went ahead to the castle that belonged to the ogre, who was the true owner of the land. He was a very rich ogre with special powers.

When Puss got to the castle, he asked to see the ogre.

When he was brought before the ogre, Puss boldly said, "I have heard of your great powers to change yourself into any animal at all, even a lion or an elephant!"

"It is true," roared the ogre, as he changed into the form of a fearsome lion. The terrified Puss leaped up onto a cupboard. He jumped down when the ogre turned himself back into an ogre.

Puss lied to the ogre and said that he was very frightened. Then he said, "I have heard that you can also change yourself into a tiny animal, even a mouse. But that's impossible!"

"What? Impossible?!" roared the ogre. "Not impossible for me!" In the blink of an eye, he changed himself into a little gray mouse.

Puss wasted no time. He pounced on the mouse and ate it. As the mouse was gone, so was the ogre.

Meanwhile, the king's coach had arrived at the castle. Just as the king asked whose castle it was, Puss ran out to welcome the king and the princess. Puss said, "Welcome to the castle of the duke of Carabas!"

"Don't tell me this fine castle is yours, dear duke!" exclaimed the king.

The duke merely smiled and led the king and the princess into the great hall.

The king, the princess, the duke, and Puss enjoyed a splendid feast prepared by the ogre's servants. Then the king offered the charming duke his daughter's hand in marriage.

The duke and the princess were married that day. As for clever Puss, he lived a life of ease ever after.